TOO EXCITED TO SLEEP!

Masterful Person Company Publishing

Dedication

To my loving husband John, whose unwavering support and encouragement were foundational in the creation of this book. Your belief in my abilities has been an invaluable asset. To my little Maurion, whose presence and zest for life continually remind me of the importance of fostering imagination and nurturing dreams across generations. And to Jen Furlong, who has been an exemplary mentor and guide throughout this process. Your insights, expertise, and steadfast leadership were instrumental in navigating the journey of writing my very first book. I extend my deepest gratitude to each of you for your unique and significant role in bringing this project to life. I hope this book will serve as an inspiration and resource to the readers who hold the future in their hands. Here's to the power of perseverance, the importance of dreams, and the limitless potential within each of us. Thanks again.

~Tammy Christian

©2023 by Tammy Christian. All rights reserved.

Library of Congress Control Number: 2023916448

Summary: A young mouse is too excited to sleep at school nap time and stands up to predators who want to disrupt the peace.

Masterful Person Company Publishing
70 Willowmere Pond Rd Stafford VA
22556
www.mpcpublishing.com

TOO EXCITED TO SLEEP!

By Tammy Christian

Illustrated By Jiya Daim

Once upon a time there was a little mouse named Jack.

Jack loved school. He loved playing with his friends.

He loved playing with all the toys his teacher, Mrs. Peacock, kept in the classroom.

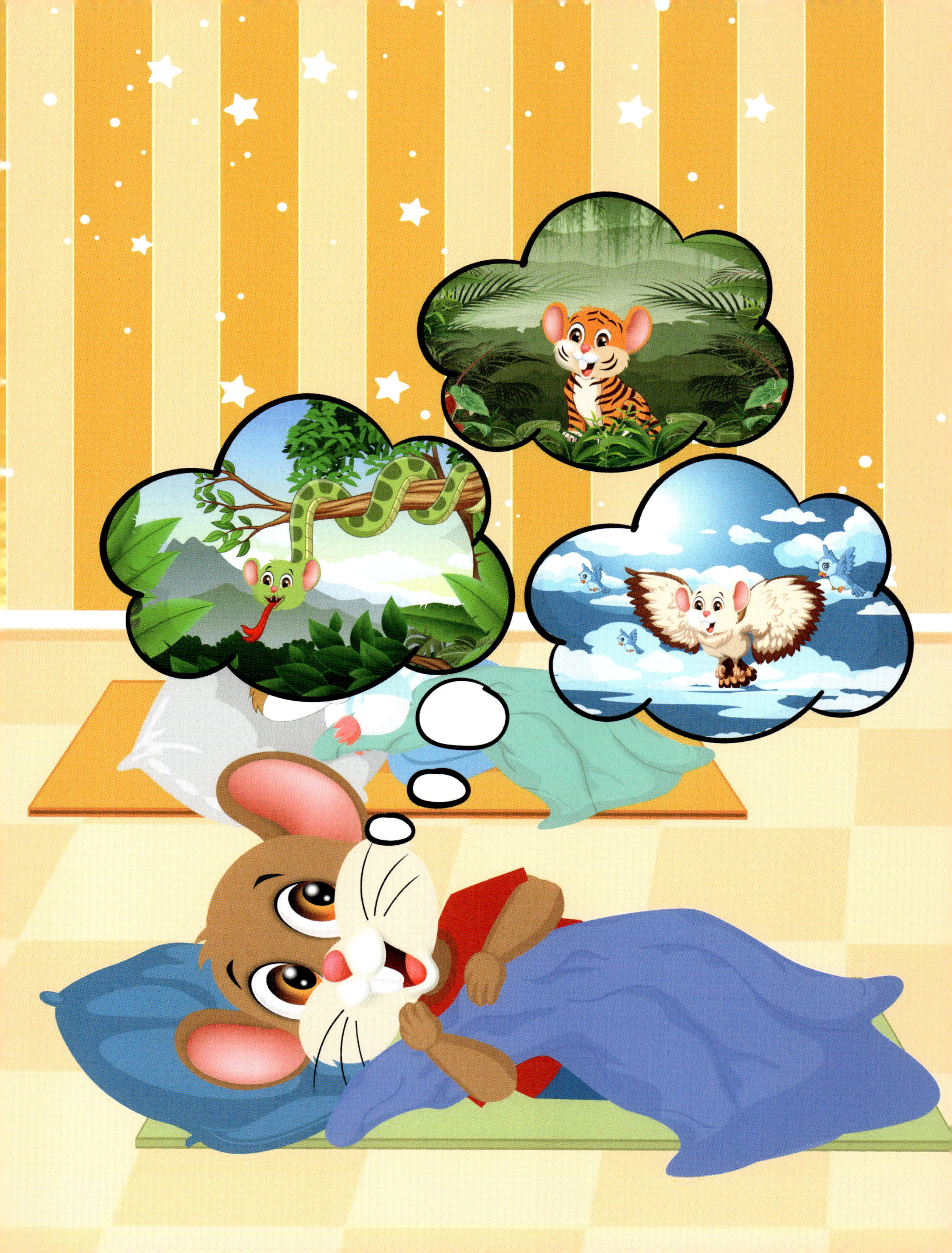

Jack loved school so much that when nap time came, he was too excited to sleep. Jack tossed and turned. He imagined he was a bird gliding through the air. He imagined he was a tiger prowling the jungle. He imagined he was a python squeezing the branch of a tree.

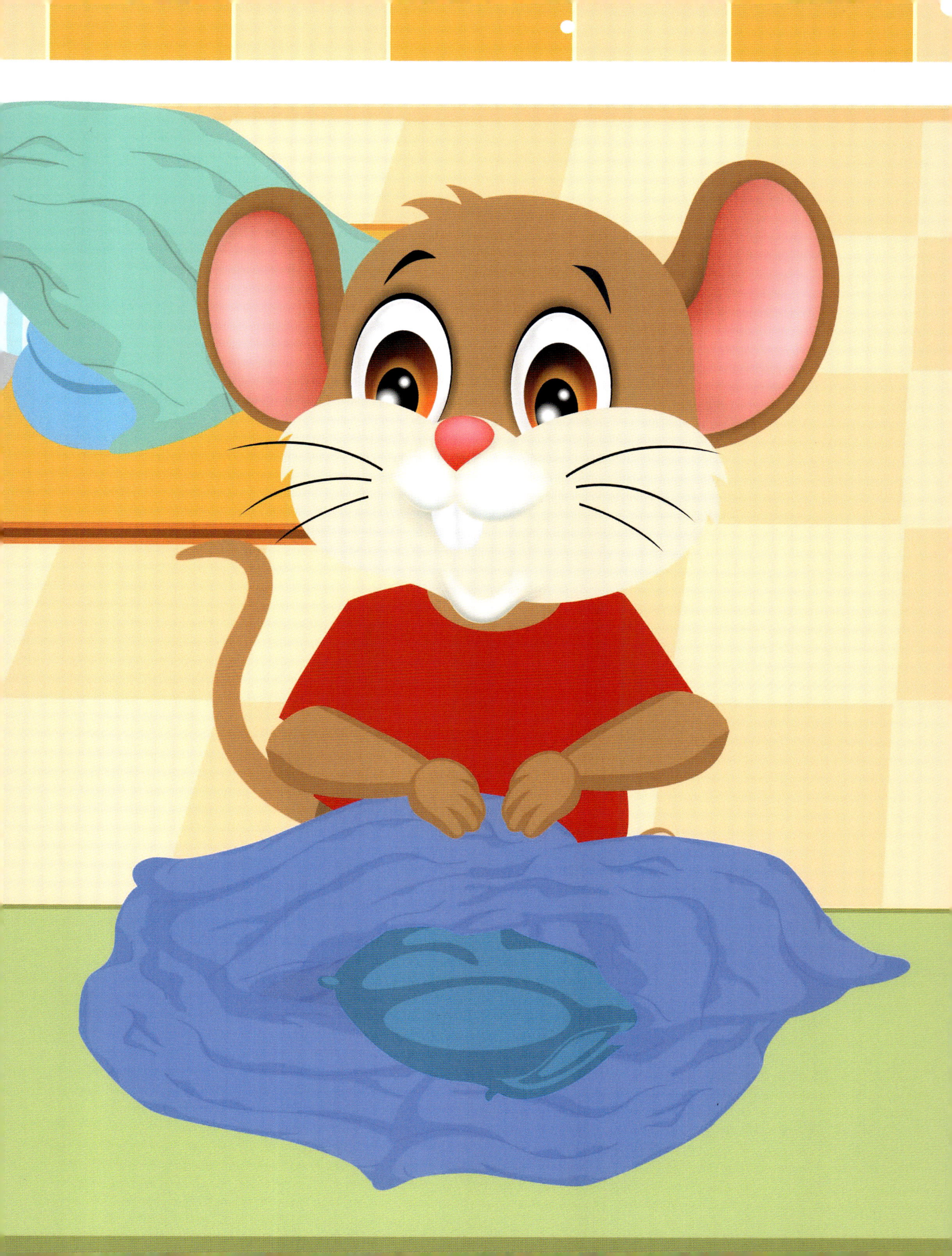

Jack made a nest out of his pillow and blanket. He was too excited to sleep!

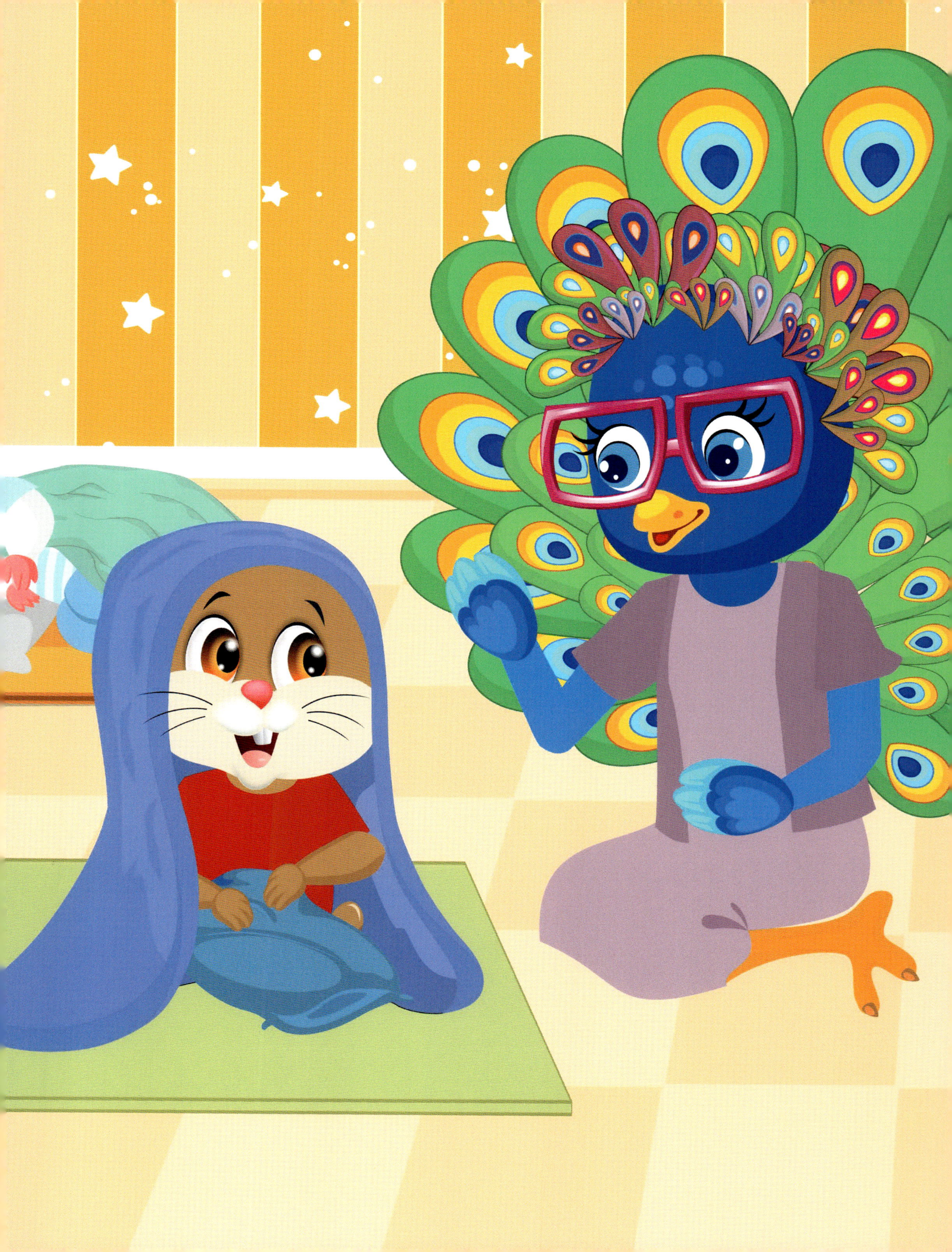

"What's wrong, Jack?" asked Mrs. Peacock. "Don't you want to sleep?"

"Squeak, squeak, I'm too excited to sleep!"

"Now Jack," said Mrs. Peacock, "sleep keeps you strong and healthy. Won't you give it a try?" Jack let out a big yawn.

"Squeak, squeak. I'm too excited to sleep!"

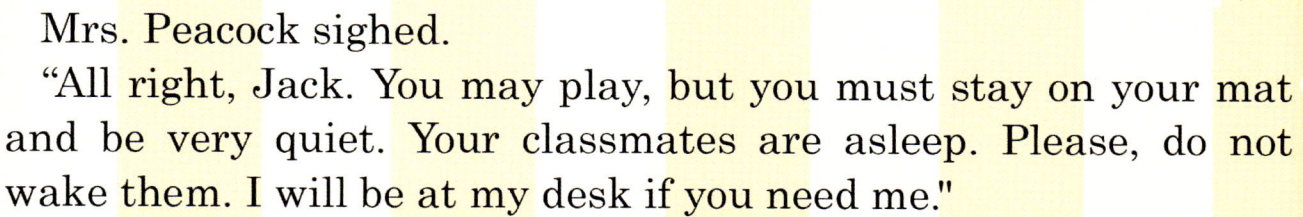

Mrs. Peacock sighed.

"All right, Jack. You may play, but you must stay on your mat and be very quiet. Your classmates are asleep. Please, do not wake them. I will be at my desk if you need me."

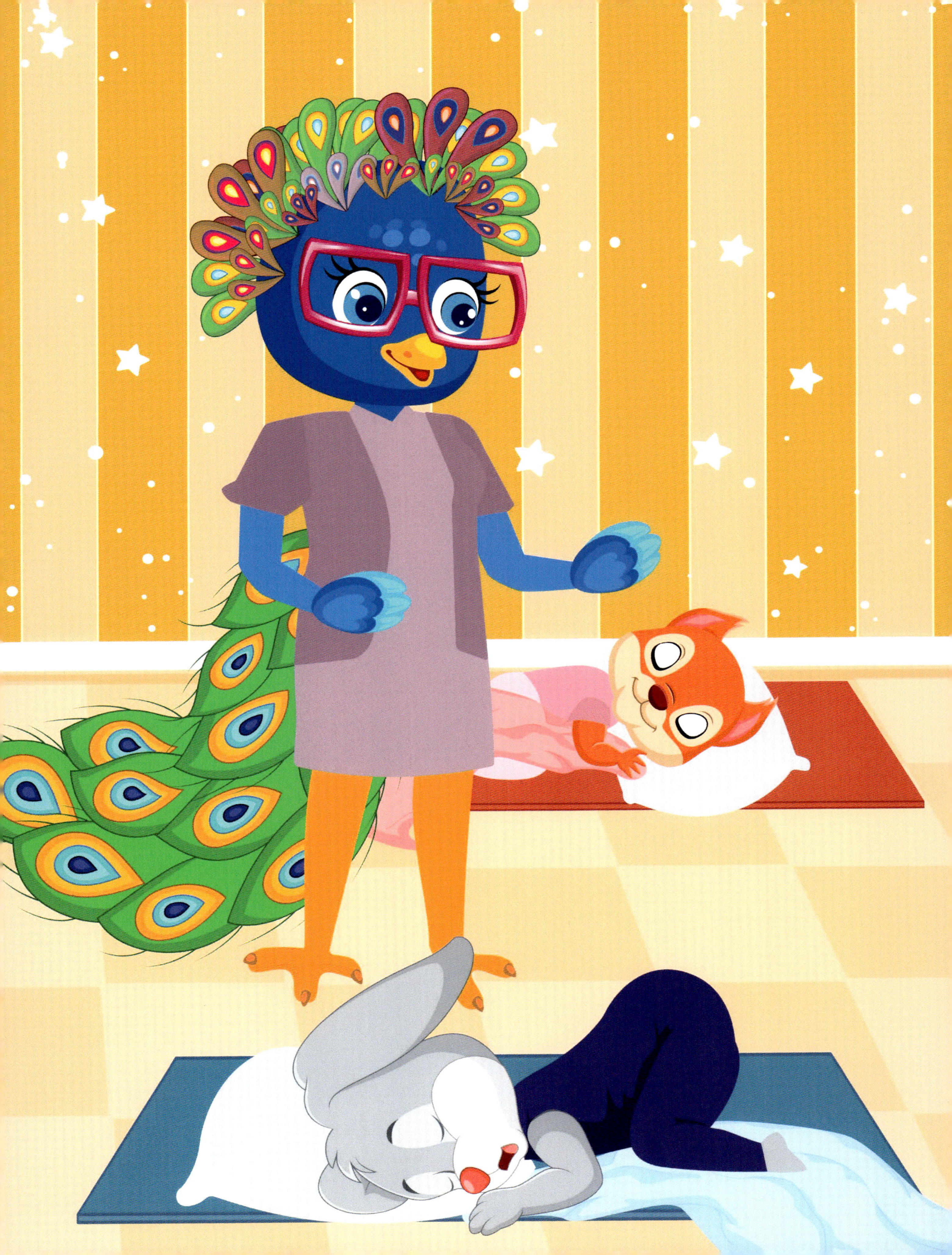

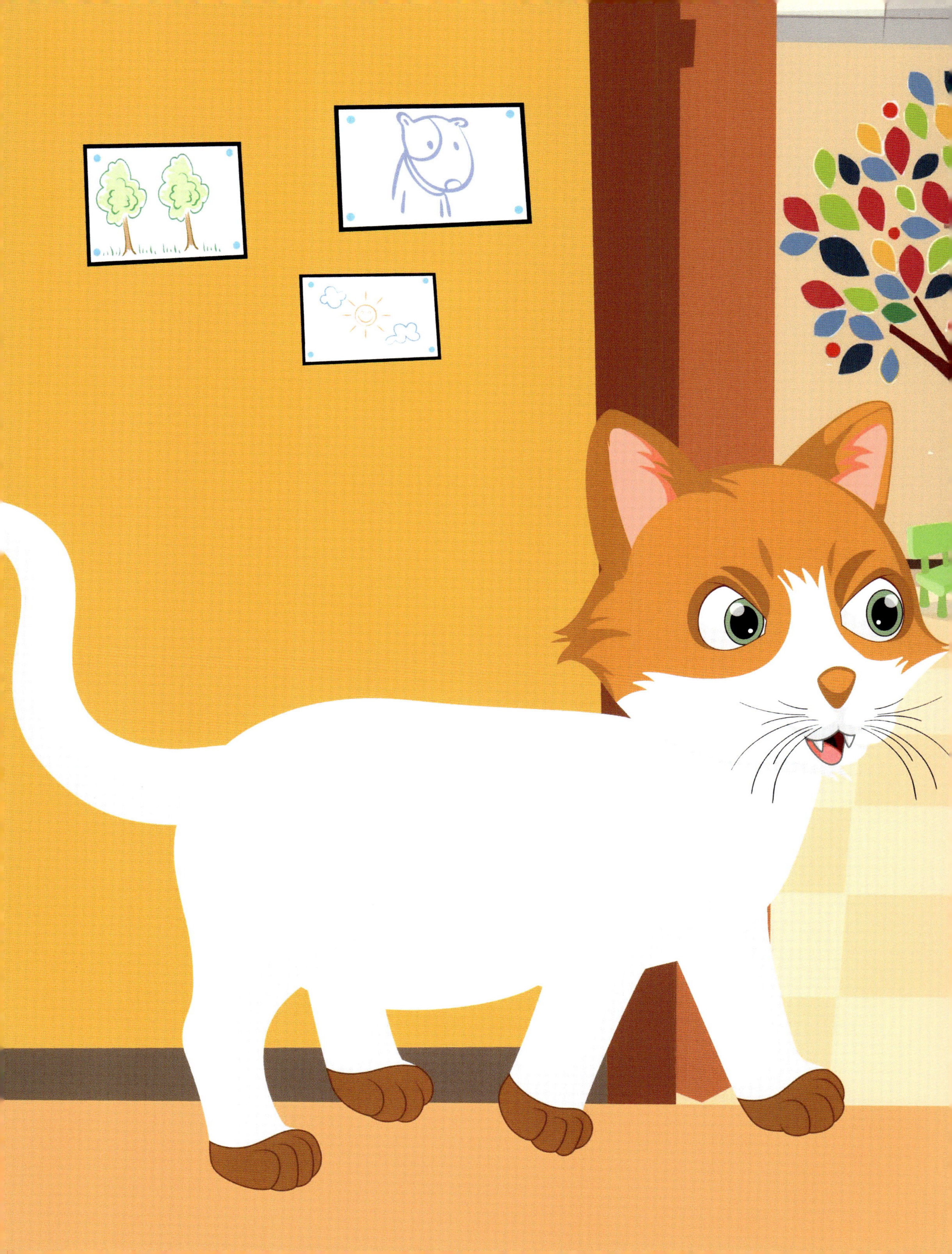

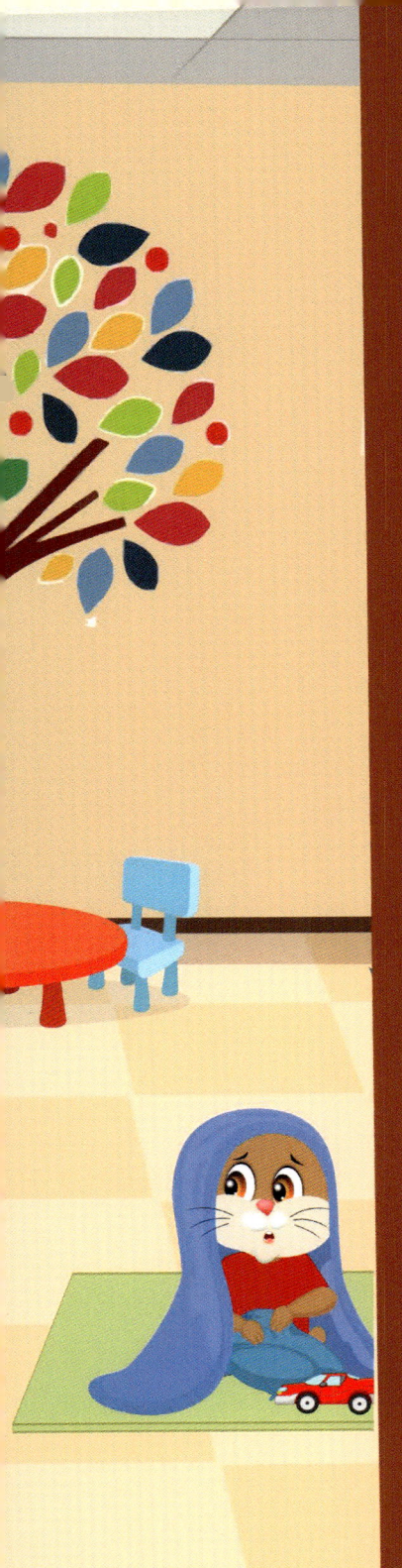

Jack did his best to play quietly. A loud, creaking sound made him look up. A sly cat prowled back and forth in front of the classroom door.

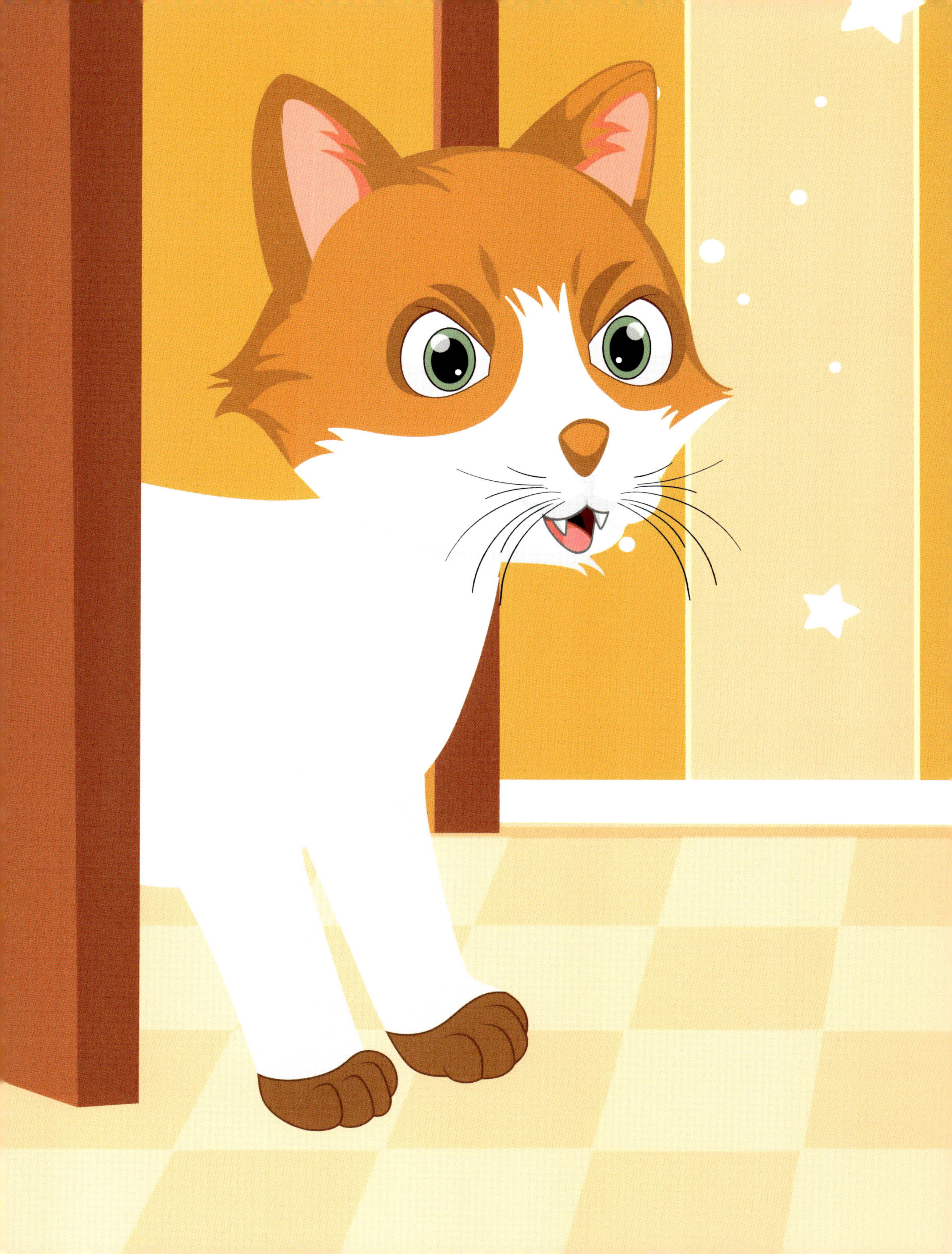

"Meow, little mouse," said the sly cat.

"Shh!" whispered Jack. "My classmates are napping and you must not wake them!"

"If they are sleeping, why are you awake?"

"Squeak, squeak! I'm too excited to sleep."

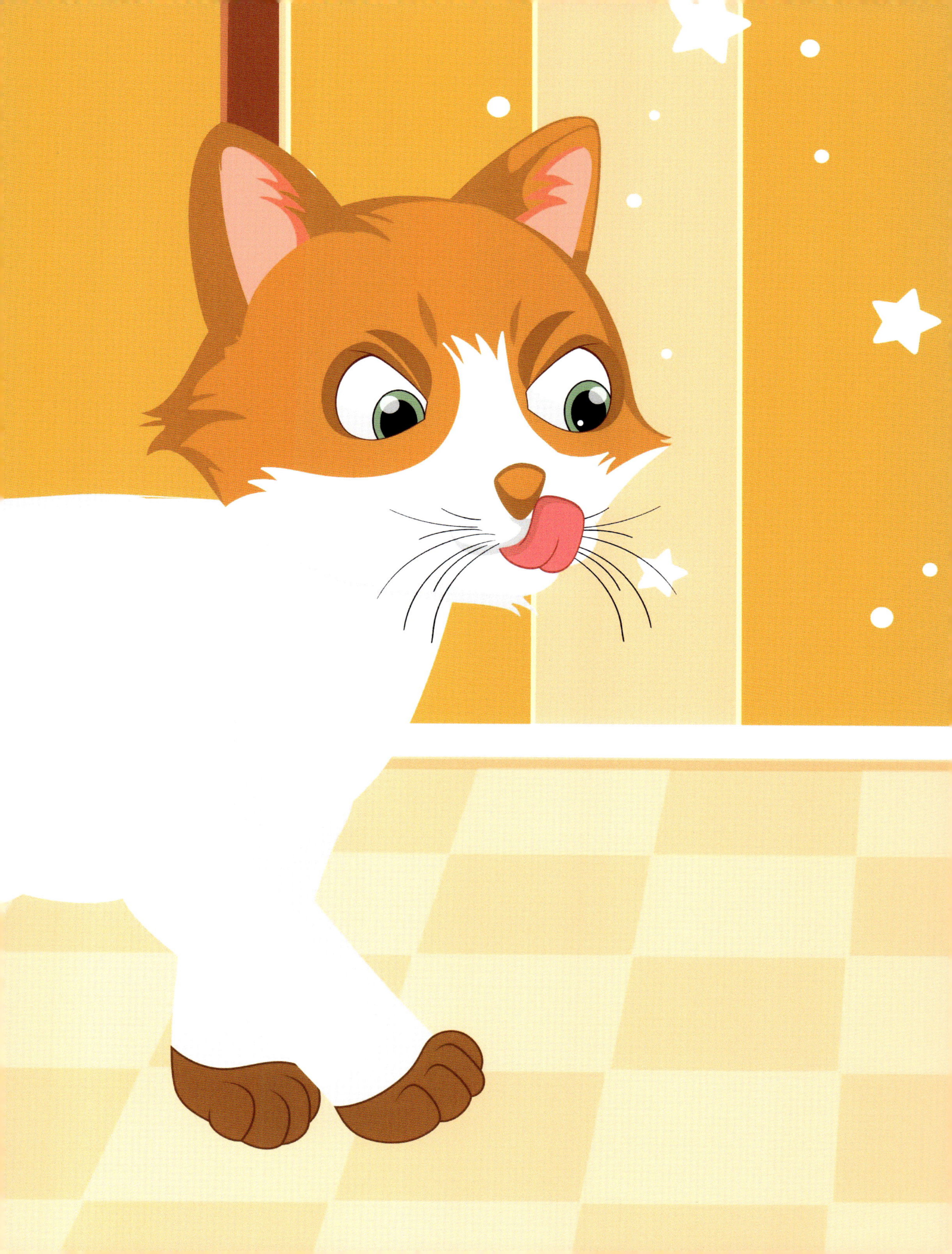

"I can help with that," he purred. "Just walk into my mouth. It's dark here. You'll be asleep in no time!"

"No, thank you," said Jack. "I'm supposed to play quietly on my mat."

The sly cat licked his lips and crept closer. Jack stood firm before the cat. He would make sure his friends stayed asleep.

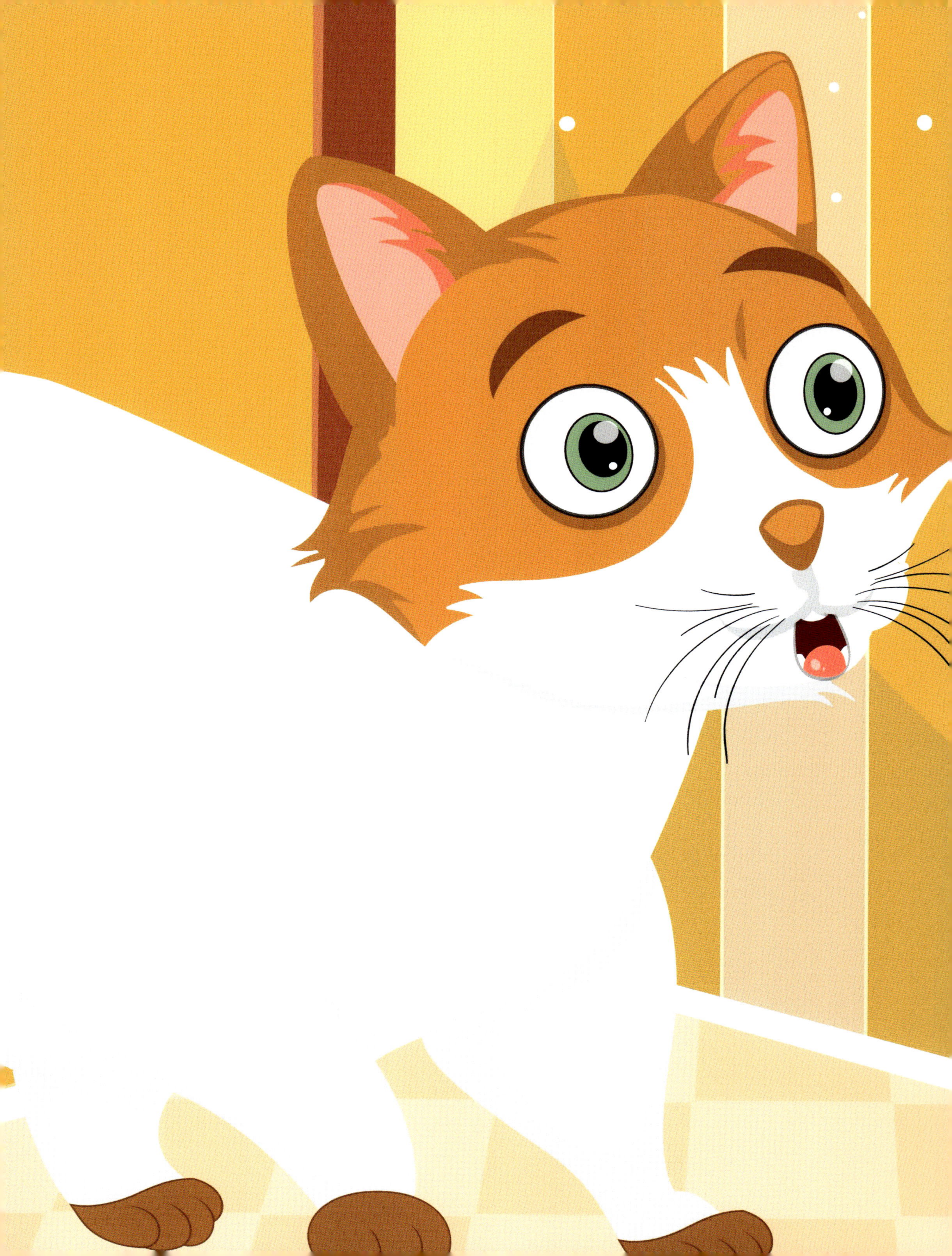

A cool shadow brushed Jack's shoulder. The sly cat's eyes went wide. He shot like a race car out the door. Jack turned to see what scared the cat, but the shadow was gone.

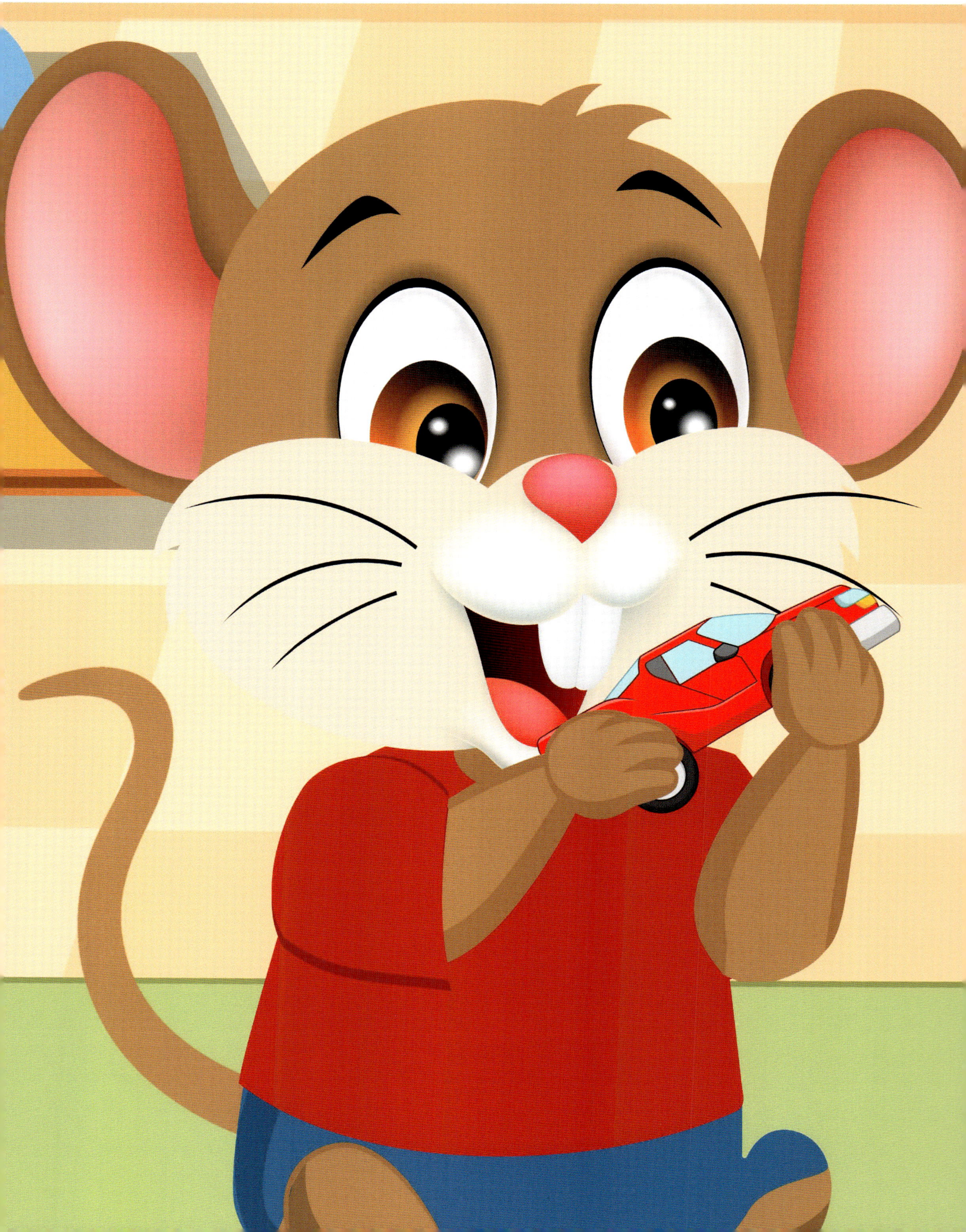

Jack returned to playing with his toys. A husky sliding sound made him look up.

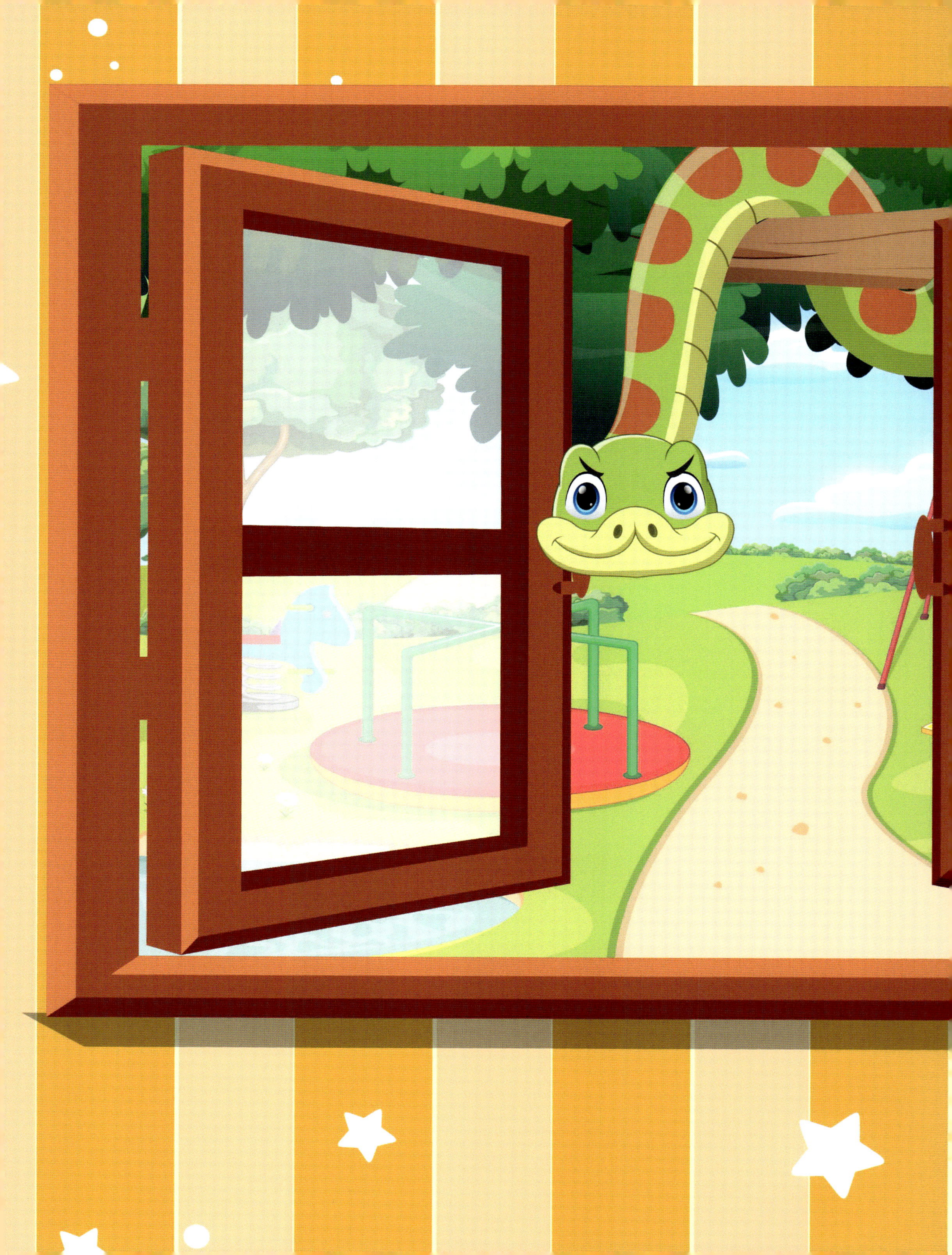

A spotted snake slithered through the open window.

"Why aren't you sssleeping?" hissed the snake.

Jack let out a big yawn.

"Squeak, squeak! I'm too excited to sleep."

The snake flicked his tongue.
"The breeze from the window is making you cold. You could climb into my coils. I would keep you warm. Then you can sleep."

"No, thank you," Jack said. "I'm supposed to play quietly on my mat." The snake offered its coils again. Jack stood his ground.

"Go away," whispered Jack. He pointed at the window. The snake slid closer.

Then, a cool shadow brushed Jack's shoulder. The spotted snake froze, then slithered back out the window as fast as he could. Jack turned to see what frightened the snake, but the shadow was gone.

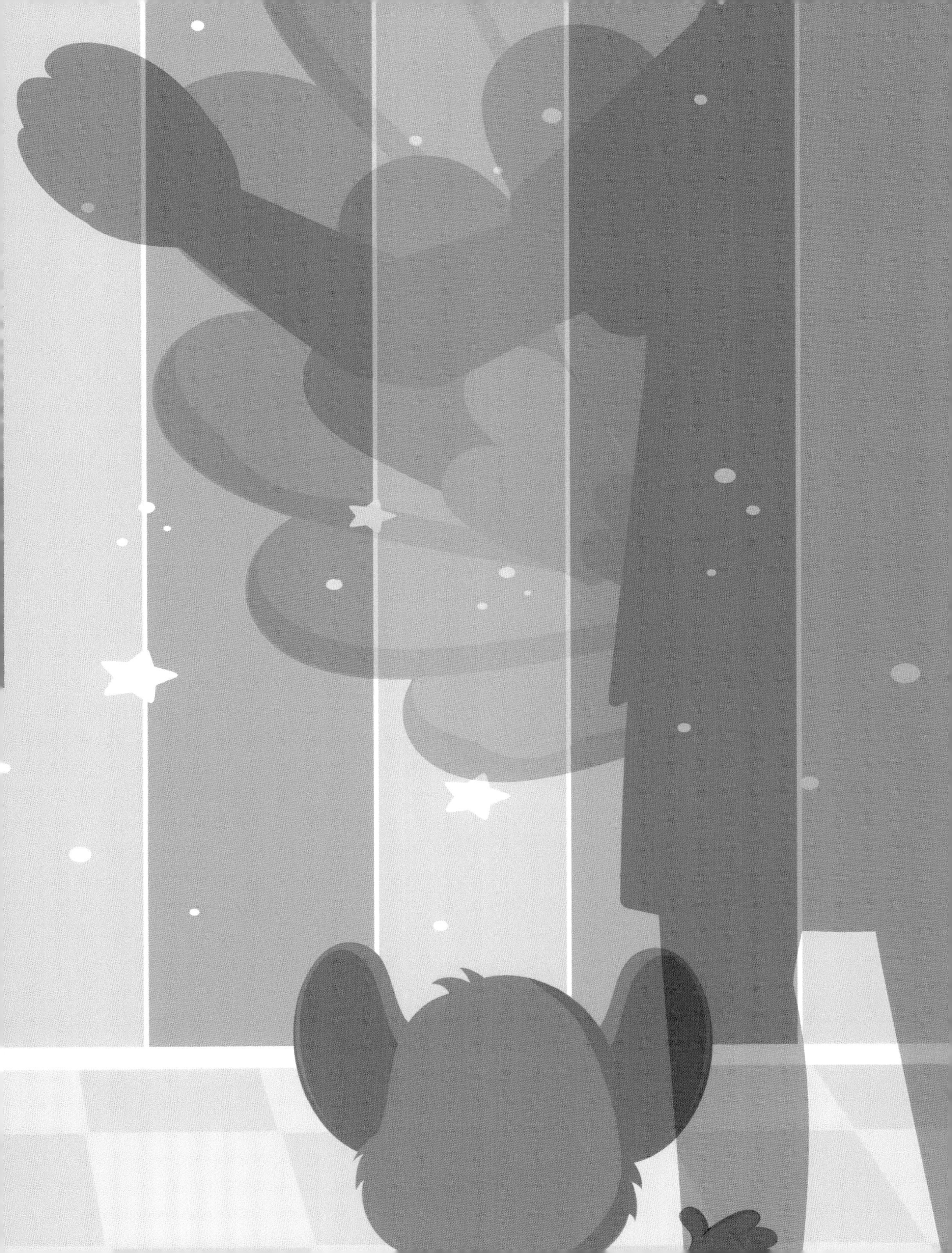

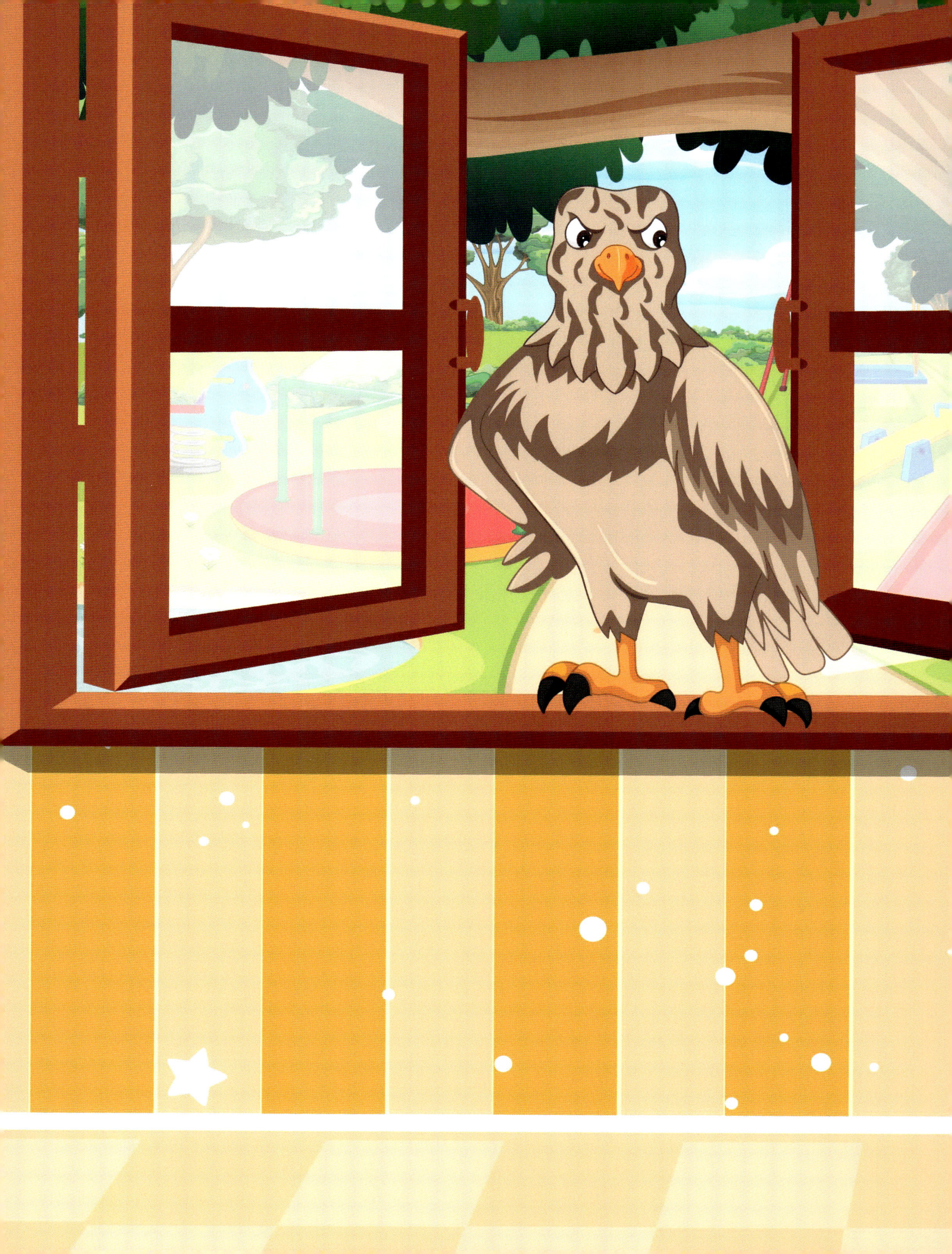

A moment later, Jack heard the beat of powerful wings.

"Why aren't you sleeping?" asked a feathery hawk.

"Shh!" whispered Jack. "Squeak, squeak, I'm too excited to sleep."

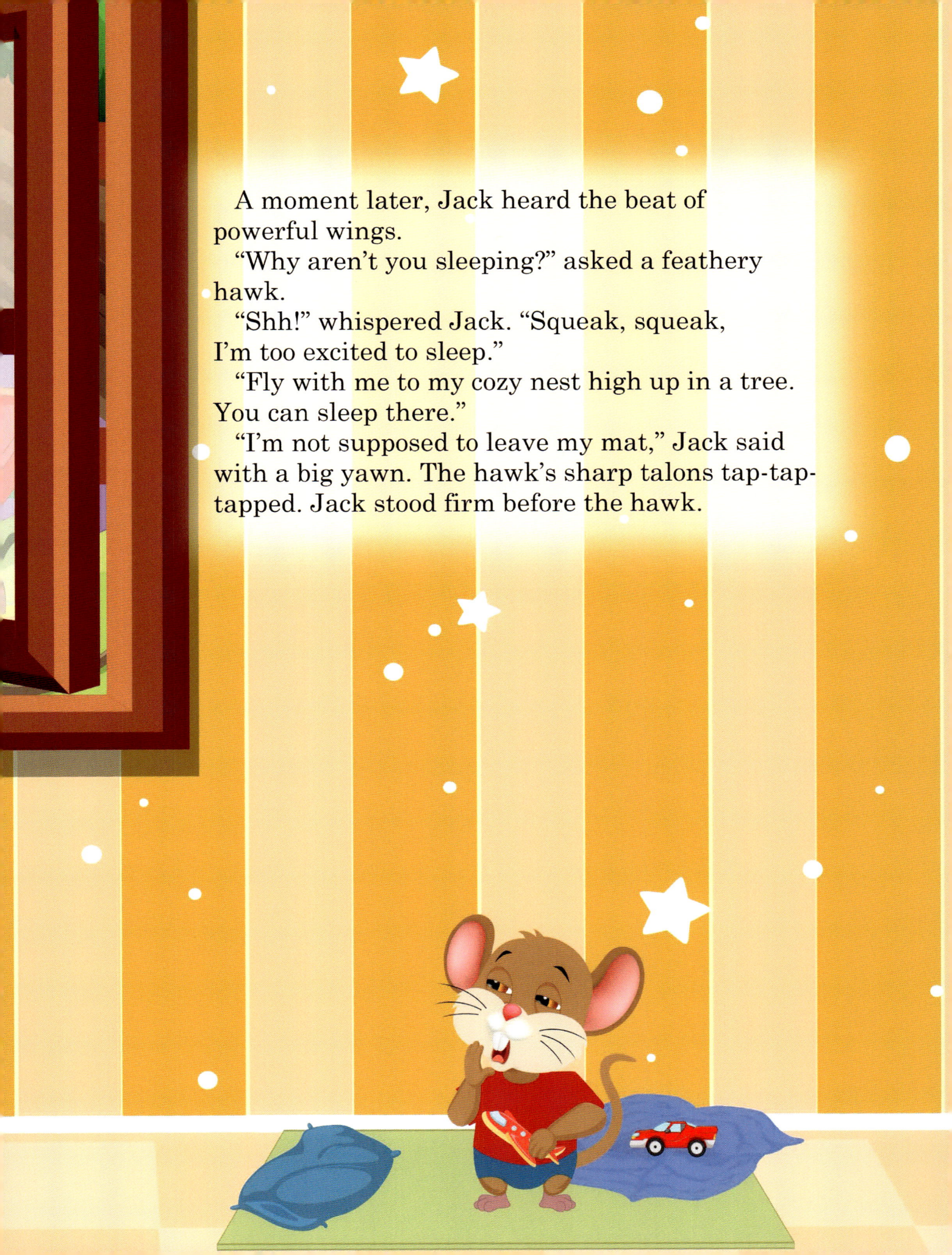

"Fly with me to my cozy nest high up in a tree. You can sleep there."

"I'm not supposed to leave my mat," Jack said with a big yawn. The hawk's sharp talons tap-tap-tapped. Jack stood firm before the hawk.

Suddenly, the feathery hawk opened his wings wide. Mrs. Peacock leapt from behind Jack and flapped her huge wings. The hawk screeched and flew away.

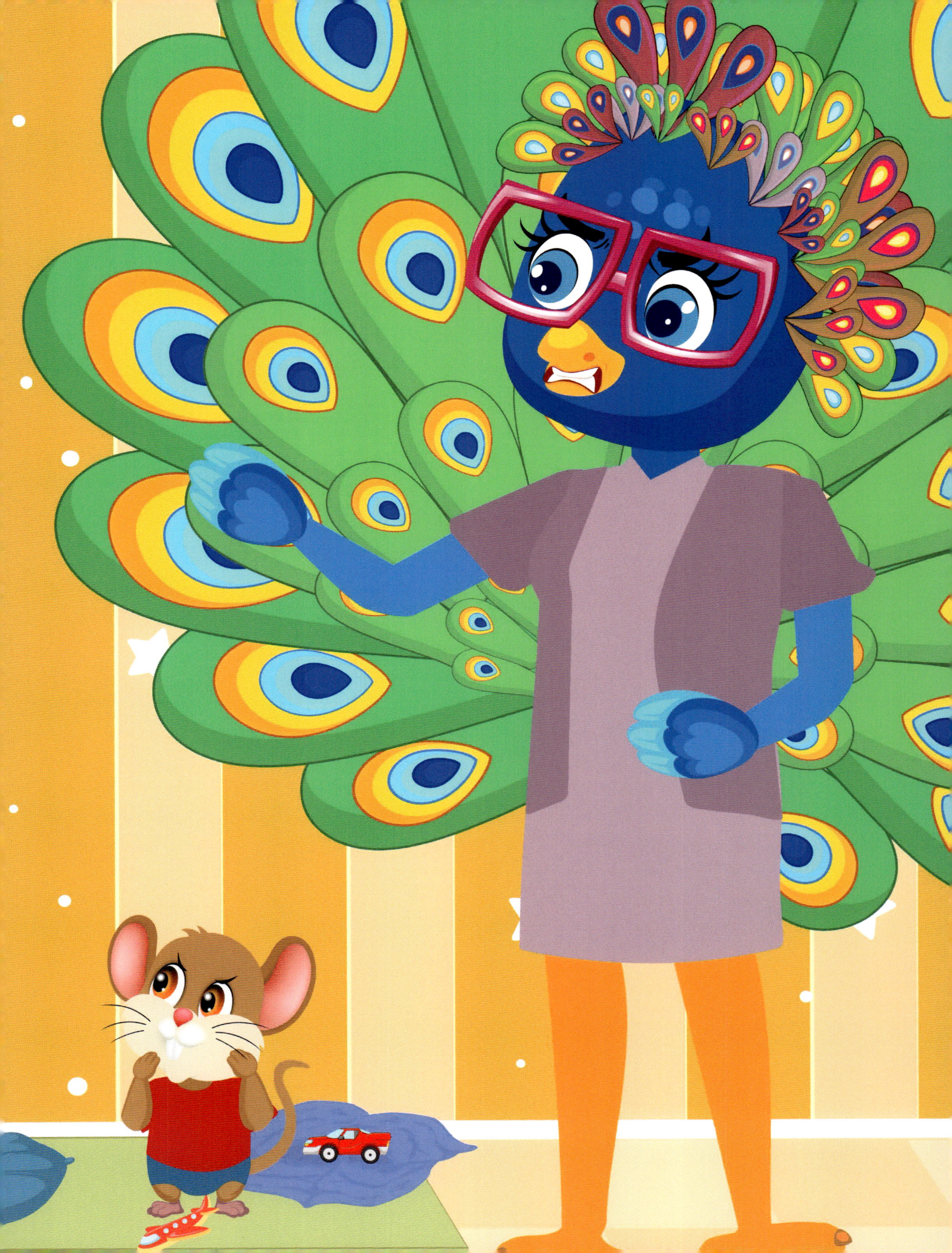

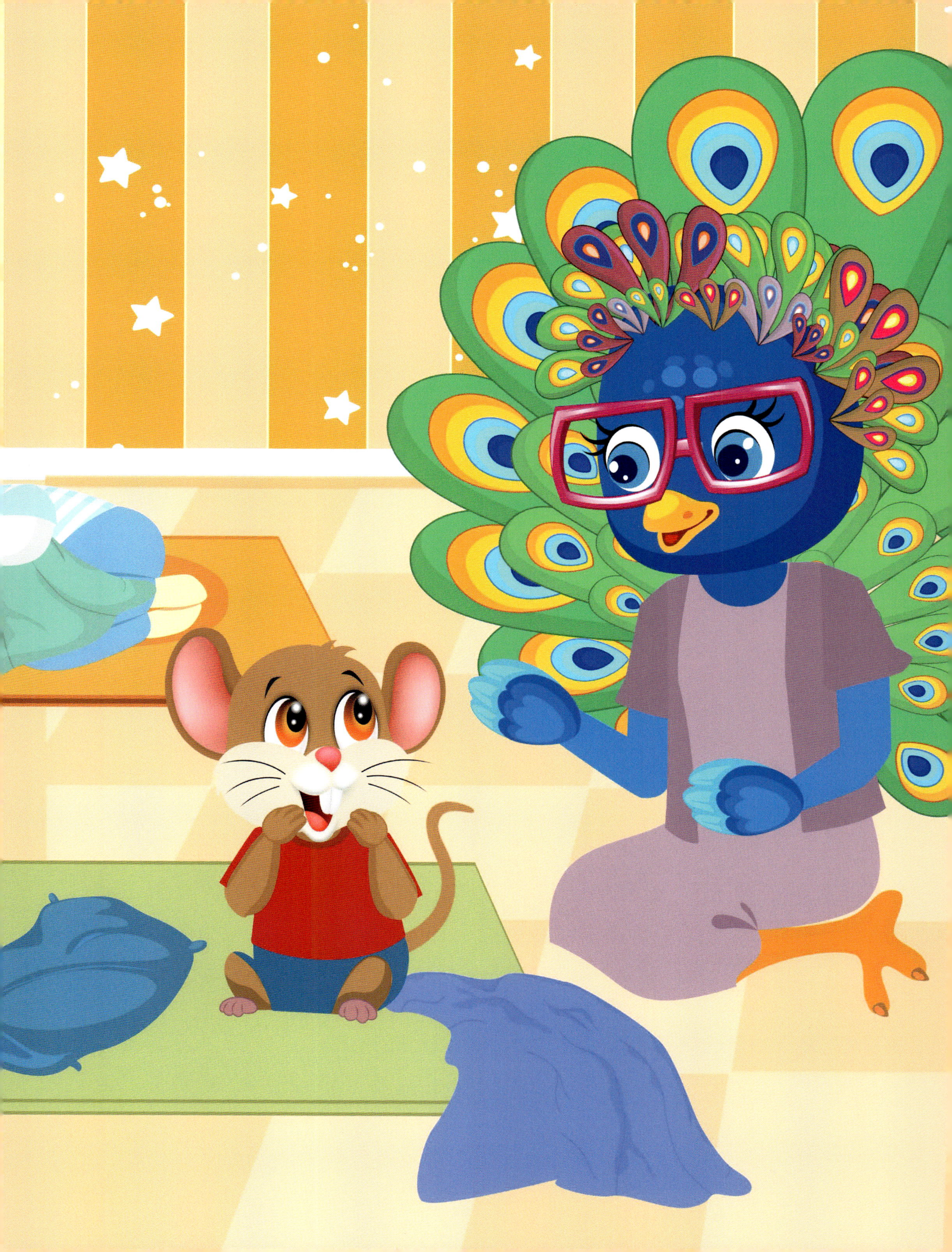

"Jack!" said Mrs. Peacock. "Are you okay?"
Jack nodded. "Yes! Were you there all the time?"
"Yes, I was, Jack," said Mrs. Peacock.

When Jack's mom picked him up that afternoon, he couldn't wait to tell her about his day.

"Mommy," squeaked Jack. "I was too excited to sleep at nap time. Some animals wanted me to leave my classroom, but I said no!"

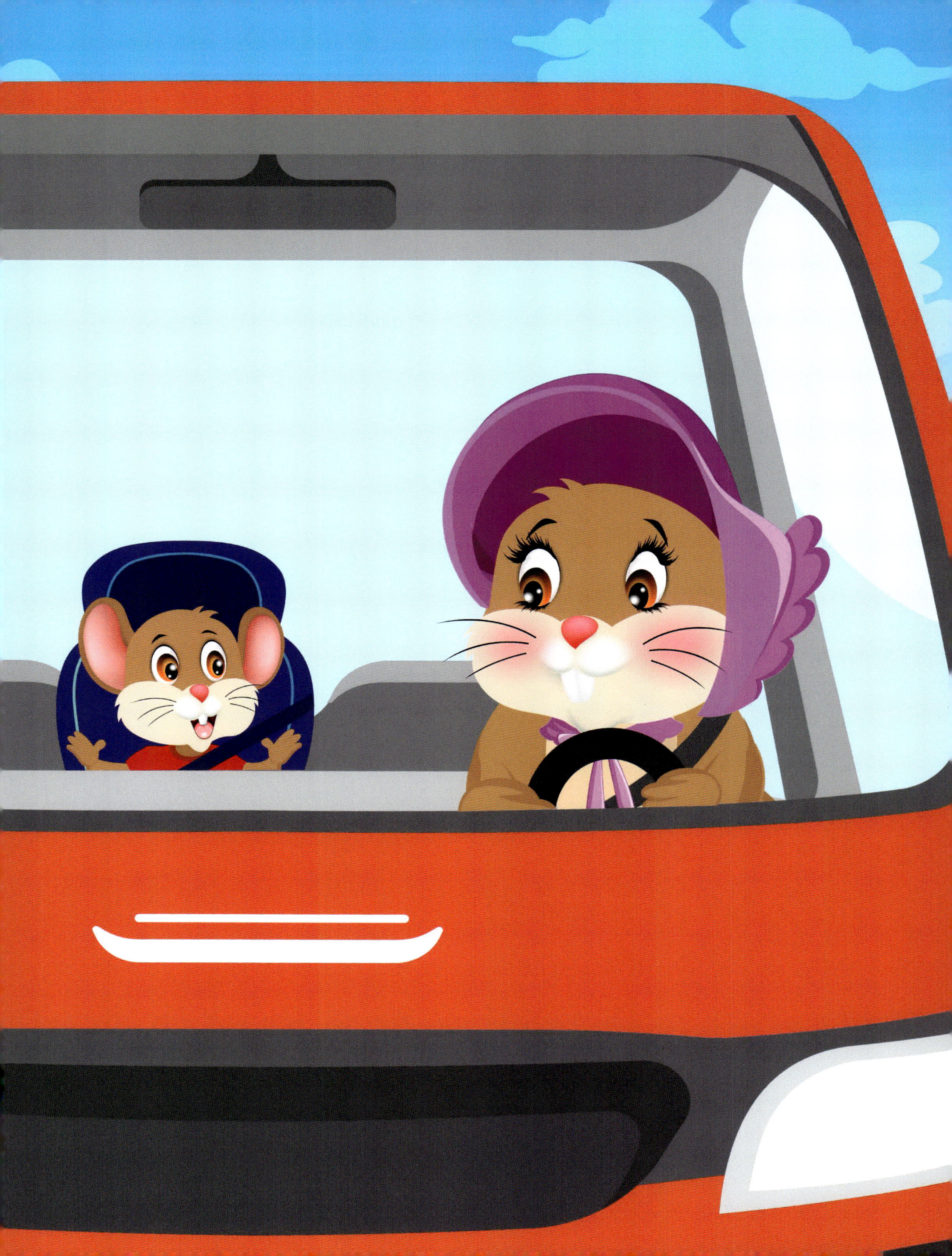

Jack's mom looked worried for a moment, then she smiled. "You did a good thing by not going with them, Jack, but why didn't you want to rest?"
   "Because there were so many fun things to do at school, I didn't want to miss them." Jack's mom laughed.
   "Sleep makes you healthy and strong. If you take your naps, you won't miss out on anything. You'll have energy to do more fun things like play outside with your friends. How about you rest tomorrow during nap time? Jack? Jack? Are you listening?"

But Jack wasn't listening. He had fallen fast asleep.

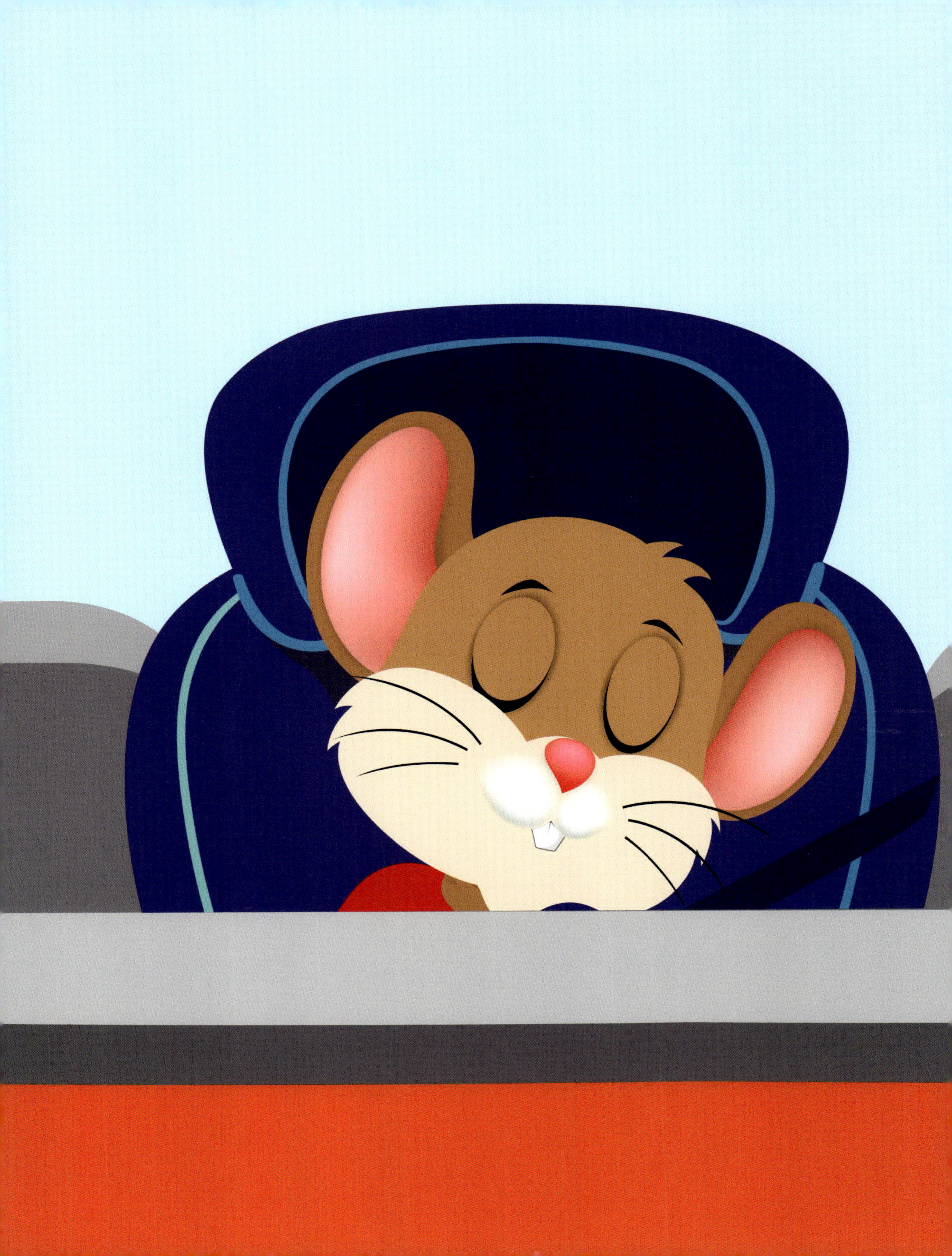

The End.

ABOUT THE AUTHOR

Tammy Christian is a wife and mother from Northern Virginia. By day, she is an IT Sr. Systems Administrator. She loves dancing, vegetarian cooking, and collecting dolls. She eagerly awaits Friday night board games with her family. Too Excited to Sleep is her debut picture book.

Find out more at tammycauthor.com

ABOUT THE ILLUSTRATOR

Jiya Daim is an illustrator who finds magic in bringing imaginary characters to life. She creates colorful drawings that make kids want to read more. She enjoys crafting, painting, badminton, and supporting her family.

Follow me on IG @childrenbooksillustrator